Schnoodle Shenanigans!

A Surprise Birthday Party

JILL E. BEAN

LifeRich Publishing is a registered trademark of The Reader's Digest Association, Inc.

LifeRich Publishing books may be ordered through booksellers or by contacting:

LifeRich Publishing
1663 Liberty Drive
Bloomington, IN 47403
www.liferichpublishing.com
844-686-9607

Because of the dynamic nature of the Internet, any web addresses or links contained in this book may have changed since publication and may no longer be valid. The views expressed in this work are solely those of the author and do not necessarily reflect the views of the publisher, and the publisher hereby disclaims any responsibility for them.

Any people depicted in stock imagery provided by Getty Images are models, and such images are being used for illustrative purposes only. Certain stock imagery © Getty Images.

Scripture taken from the Holy Bible, NEW INTERNATIONAL VERSION®. Copyright © 1973, 1978, 1984, 2011 by Biblica, Inc. All rights reserved worldwide. Used by permission. NEW INTERNATIONAL VERSION® and NIV® are registered trademarks of Biblica, Inc. Use of either trademark for the offering of goods or services requires the prior written consent of Biblica US, Inc.

ISBN: 978-1-4897-4738-9 (sc)
ISBN: 978-1-4897-4737-2 (hc)
ISBN: 978-1-4897-4739-6 (e)

Print information available on the last page.

LifeRich Publishing rev. date: 02/28/2024

Schnoodle Shenanigans!

A Surprise Birthday Party

Chapter 1
On a Birthday Mission

Table of Contents

I'm Tucker, and I'm a schnoodle. That means I'm part poodle and part schnauzer, but 100 percent goofy. The morning alarm clock just went off, signaling the exciting start to a brand-new day.

I howl along to let my little people know it's time to get up! There are three of them: Paul, Makaila, and Hannah.

Skipping downstairs for breakfast, I wear a big, furry grin. My pointed ears are always bouncing and waving hello! I have curly-whirly fur and a long, pink tongue that doesn't quite fit in my mouth.

I look like I'm always blowing a raspberry! The best, though, is my nose! It smells *everything!*

I've learned to use my nose like a lever to open the pantry door, the garbage door, and the back door. Some of the best things are just waiting behind doors. When I can't resist the delicious smells, I go through the garbage. That's when my people call me "Mr. Tucker" with a stern voice! Sometimes they put the Schnoodelizer 2000 through the garbage door handles so I can't lever them open. The little pokey parts go up my nose and keep me out of the forbidden scraps. Funny, though—I see them use the Schnoodelizer 2000 to scoop spaghetti from the pot onto their plates!

Heading to the pantry, I lever the door open with my handy nose. I sniff through my breakfast options until I settle on pancakes with maple syrup and bacon. Lots and lots of bacon!

 It doesn't seem to matter how much I tell my people what I want for breakfast—all they hear is *woof, woof, woof,* and they give me dry, round kibbles.

After I get up, then my people get up, and always, always last is Molly. Molly is the other dog in my house, and she is older than I am. She organizes and runs the house and our people. Molly is a small ball of white fluff, but don't let that fool you. When I don't listen, Molly shows me her teeth and vibrates with growls. She takes long, lazy naps in her cozy dog bed once our people are busy for the day. Crunching my kibble, little crumbles fly out of my mouth in every direction. I glance up to see all my people at the breakfast table. Mom and Dad are sipping out of hot, steaming mugs, their eyes still half-closed. I don't know why they like it so much. It smells terrible to me.

Paul is eating and trying to finish his homework. Pieces of bagel and jam sprinkle the floor beneath the table. Most days it's a shower of tasty tidbits. Other times, when Mom cooks liver, there is a steady downpour of meat. Makaila is building a house by stacking her toast and coating it in peanut butter. Yum! Now that smells delicious. I wonder if I could have part of that toast house. Hannah is sitting politely, swinging her legs under the table, and swirling her cereal in the bowl.

She would probably share with me. Circling past Hannah, I scoop up cereal on the floor.

Mom is finally finished with that bitter-smelling drink in her mug. It's amazing; her eyes are wide open! Today is Molly's birthday, and we are giving her a surprise party. Mom shows me the list with cake, ice cream, and decorations that we need. She rolls it up and tucks it into my collar. Mom whispers, "You're a good boy, Tucker! I know I can trust you to get all of Molly's birthday supplies in town." I give Mom a lopsided grin and howl with joy. I can be trusted! I am on the job! I push the back door with my nose and bounce out toward town.

What a day! The air smells like popcorn and squirrels throughout the park. Popcorn Man sells his buttery, salted treats in the center of the park. I like crunching the kernels that fall from his cart and hide in the grass.

The freshly mowed grass feels soft and cool against my paws.

 A squirrel races past me, dropping acorns as he skitters up a tree.

Now, for humans, the smell of a squirrel is, well, disgusting! But to me they smell like fresh cookies baking in a hot oven.

Laser-focused on the tempting squirrel, I step into a big, squishy piece of pink bubble gum. It smooshes up between my toes. *Ick!* I try to lick it away, but it sticks and sticks. The gum is a sweet, smooshy bedroom slipper on my paw!

I put the unwanted slipper out of my mind and march forward on my birthday mission. From that moment on, my bubble gum slipper stretches out behind me like a sticky, elastic band.

What Is Sin?

Sin is what we do or think about that goes against God and His Word. The Bible is God's Word. It is our guide that tells us what is right and what is sin.

Sin is always tempting; it draws us toward it. It looks inviting and sounds like a great idea. It may even smell amazing. Sin usually feels exciting while we are sinning, but afterward, we feel guilty or bad.

For example, in Tucker's doggie world, he is tempted toward the delicious-smelling garbage. He wants to go through the scraps *so* much! The smell is incredible, and playing in the garbage is fun. When Tucker gives into the temptation, he crosses the safety zone into sin. He levers open the garbage door and pulls the scraps out. He drags the delightful-smelling tidbits across the floor and eats the best ones!

In our people world, we all cross over the safety zone of temptation and into sin. Everyday, each one of us sins. This is why all of us need God's forgiveness. When we feel the pang of guilt, that is God's way of letting us know that we have sinned. Once we know that we have sinned, we can tell God about it. This is called confessing our sin. When we confess our sin, God will always forgive us.

If we confess our sins, he is faithful and just and will forgive us our sins and purify us from all unrighteousness. (1 John 1:9)

Takeaway: Sin goes against God and His Word. All of us sin and need His forgiveness.

Chapter 2
Tucker Takes the Cake!

With squirrels on my mind, I pad past the fountain in the town square. The cobblestones are smooth beneath my paws, and the spray from the fountain spritzes, tickling my nose. The bakery is just ahead. My mouth is beginning to water at the smells floating out the open windows and door.

Strawberries and whipped cream! I love whipped cream! It's so fluffy. Paul, Makaila, and Hannah sneak it to me. They like to giggle and watch me swipe the sweetened clouds off my nose with my tongue.

I smell chocolate. Wait! With my nose pointed straight up, I breathe deeply. *Sniff, sniff, sniff.* Double-chocolate fudge! Ooh, toasted marshmallow and butterscotch caramel. Yum! Maybe I could lever open their pantry and get a few samples.

The baker is waving at me. "Hello, Tucker."

I give my best smile and howl back, "Hello."

She rubs the top of my head and scratches my ears. Her hands smell like sugary doughnuts.

My mouth waters even more.

I wonder what I would look like with a doughnut hat. That could be handy! I could flip them off my head and eat them when I'm hungry!

"Tucker, would you like to ice Molly's name on top of the cake?" the sugary-smelling baker asks.

"Yes, yes!" I woof, then add, "Can I taste test it too?" But all she hears is *bark, bark, bark*. Can't she tell I'm starved?

All I've eaten today is kibble. I sit politely with my good-boy smile, droop my eyes downward, and look extra sad.

"Oh, Tucker, are you hungry, you poor boy?"

Bingo! She gets the hint. I whimper so she knows I'm extra hungry. The sugary baker breaks apart a cookie and offers it to me.

I lick her hand clean!

Cinnamon, oatmeal, and butter. Maybe she needs help tidying up scraps from the floor behind the counter. I could come by every day while my kids are at school and help. I like to be helpful!

I climb onto a rickety wooden stool. Balancing like a tightrope walker, I reach the top of the triple-layer treat. The stool sways and tips, but I catch my balance. Teetering, I hold my breath and squeeze the icing bag until a stream of purple comes out. Little bits spray all around me, even landing on my tongue. It is lip-smacking good! Carefully, I do my very best printing to spell out Molly's name. It looks fantastic! Molly will love the swirls and polka dots. Howling with approval, I inspect the cake from all sides. That's when I tumble down from my perch into Sugar Lady's arms. I give her a big, slurpy kiss of thanks on the cheek.

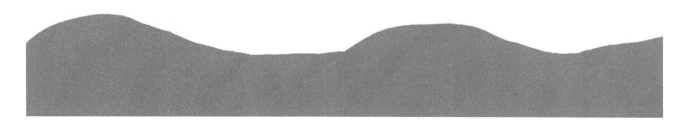

Sugar Lady carefully packs Molly's cake into a big box, then adds a string so I can carry it in my mouth. I gently pick it up and wag my tail to say, "Thank you! Goodbye! Let me know if you need help with the scraps!"

Sugar Lady calls, "Bye Tucker! See you again."

Absorbed in birthday duties, I am unaware of my smushy sponge slipper. It is firmly fitted to my paw and silently tracking me like a slithering snake.

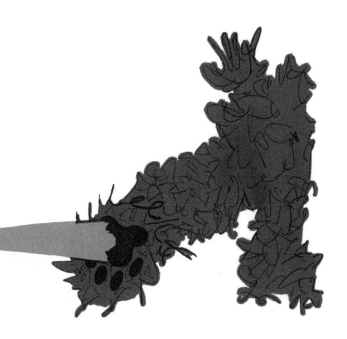

Dogs should NEVER eat chocolate, it will make them very sick. Chocolate contains caffeine, as well as a chemical that is toxic to them!

What Does Sin Look Like?

Sin is like a double-chocolate fudge cake in the bakery. The outside looks delicious with chocolate frosting and bright, colorful sprinkles. It smells so yummy that it makes our mouths water. It doesn't seem bad or hurtful in any way. Then, when a bite is taken of the amazing looking cake, it tastes like mud! A thick, yucky, mud cake that makes our stomachs sick.

Sin is tempting, like the outside of the cake. It draws us toward it because it looks or seems exciting or fun. Once we bite into it though, it becomes harmful and horrible to taste. We wish we had never taken the bite and want to wash the taste out of our mouths.

Sin reveals itself as thoughts and feelings. Sometimes it's bold, so we can recognize it or see it right away. Other times it creeps in quietly without us noticing it.

In Tucker's doggie world, he loves the mouth-watering scent of chocolate. The chocolate is like sin. The smell of it is tempting, but if Tucker eats it, he will get very sick and will need to go to his veterinarian. Chocolate is toxic to dogs, just as sin is damaging to us. All of us need God's help to recognize sin and His strength to turn away from its temptation.

And lead us not into temptation, but deliver us from evil. (Matthew 6:13)

Takeaway: Sin is tempting. Sin is always hurtful to us,
no matter what it looks or seems like.

Chapter 3
Fire Hall Fun!

Balancing the string in my teeth, it feels like dental floss sliding back and forth. Paul always says that it's important to take good care of your teeth. I'd like to try Dad's electric toothbrush. It looks fun, all buzzy and minty fresh.

I see my friend Dottie, the fire hall dog. Dottie is a dalmatian—polka-dotted black and white. It is nice that when I talk, she understands everything that I say, not like people.

"Hi, Tucker, what's in the box?" asks Dottie.

"Molly's birthday cake!" I say, with my mouth full of string.

"*Oh*, you better be careful," Dottie teases. "If anything happens to Molly's cake, she will be one upset little fluff ball!"

I cringe at the thought and gently set the stringed box off to the side.

Thinking it feels like a good time to play tag, I yell, "Not it!" I run, zigzagging like a firecracker, just out of Dottie's reach.

The firefighters are outside scrubbing the giant, red fire engine. It looks like they are giving it a bubble bath! One of the firefighters is high on a shiny ladder. He calls down to me, "Hello, Tucker!"

As I turn to bark hello, I start sliding and spinning in the water. I'm like the big cleaning sponges at the car wash that twirl and swish the bugs off the windows.

I feel Dottie's paw on my tail. "You're it," she calls, racing away.

I can hear the firefighter's voice in my ears saying, "Tucker, I need some help. When you come to a stop, can you hand me the soapy sponge in the bucket?"

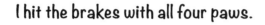 I hit the brakes with all four paws.

"Woof, woof!" Yes, I like helping! Blowing bubbles under the water with my nose, I dip deep into the foamy bucket and grab the sponge. Carefully climbing the ladder, I hand off the sponge and slide back down in the soap suds. The ladder feels slick under my paws.

A bubble works its way up my snout until I sneeze, spraying bubbles in every direction.

"Thank you, Tucker! You're a great helper!" the firefighter yells down.

"Woof, woof!" Sneeze! "Woof!" I spray a bubble cloud. "You're welcome! I have to go now."

"Make sure you get Molly's cake home safely," Dottie jokes again.

I wait until she gets close to me, then I shake water from my fur all over her. Happy with myself, I wag my tail and lift the cake box string into my mouth. "Catch you next time, Dottie!"

I do not notice my stretchy, chewy, extra gooey slipper shadowing me like a ninja.

God Forgives Us When We Ask

God will *always* freely and joyfully forgive us of our sins when we ask Him. God convicts us of sin in our lives. This conviction can cause us to feel guilty. It can also bring awareness that what we did, or thought was sinful.

God created us and loves us more than any person possibly could. He is always with us and will never leave us. He cares about every little part of our lives. God doesn't want sin to stand between us and Him.

If we want to be forgiven, all we need to do is ask God. God the Father sent His own son, Jesus, to die on the cross for our sin. Only the blood of Jesus can wash away our sin. God stands ready and willing to forgive all sin.

In Tucker's doggie world, the fire engine is grimy and represents sin. It dirties and spoils everything it touches. The firefighters work hard to wash the mess away with soapy sponges and water. God will forgive and wash us perfectly clean of all sin. The Bible says He washes us whiter than snow. There is not a speck of dirt, or sin, that is left behind.

Wash me, and I shall be whiter than snow. (Psalm 51:7)

Takeaway: God will *always* forgive you of *every* sin when you ask.

Chapter 4
Tigers! I Don't Think So!

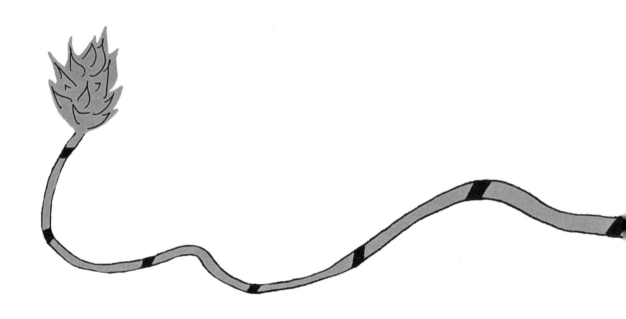

Still shaking off suds, I head for the ice cream parlor. I love ice cream! What a yummy, sweet treat! I like the way it melts into little puddles in my mouth and sticks to my whiskers. It's fun to lick off later. All those creamy whiskers are like tasty wires springing from my snout.

I push the door open, panting from the heat outside. My hot breath hits the cold air inside the ice cream parlor. It forms a white wisp that hangs in front of me. The more I pant, the more small, white puffs form and float from my mouth. Hmm, I look like a steam engine! I will unload my cargo here. Gently, I set down Molly's birthday cake.

I see my friend, Mustache Man, who scoops the ice cream. I give a howl and a long, white stream comes from my mouth, just like a train whistle.

"Hello, my friend! You're looking handsome today, and hungry. Are you hungry?" asks Mustache Man.

"I am! I am!" I bark back, and I think, *What a smart man he is*. Also, our mustaches look a lot alike. Hmm, he is handsome! I wonder if he licks leftover ice cream from his mustache too.

Oh, so many flavors! My mouth is watering again. Blue bubble gum! I bet you can really blow bubbles with it! Purple grape, pink cotton candy, red candy apple. There's even a kind that is orange with black stripes. I once heard Mustache Man say it was called tiger, but I don't think there are any tigers in that ice cream. Cats don't like the cold!

"Come, my friend! You must try my new flavor creation and tell me what you think," Moustache Man's jolly voice sings out. "It's birthday cake supreme with bits of cherry."

He lowers a bowl down to me.

I lap up the sweet treat as fast as I can. "Five out of five stars!" I bark. "My compliments to the chef!" A little part of me thinks it could use bacon sprinkles, but I don't want to be rude. "Molly will love this!" I lick the bowl so clean that I can see my face in the bottom. I have cherries stuck between my teeth!

"Good, good, my friend, I'm glad you like it." Mustache Man packs a container of the creamy dessert and ties a string around it so I can carry it. Maybe the string will floss the cherries out of my teeth! I like seeing my breath hang in the air. I give one last howl, and it's a good *long* one! I want to see if I can make the white puff reach all the way across the shop. Yes! I did it! It looks like a long line of marshmallows dancing in the air and out the door!

Do I notice my sticky, fluffy footwear? No! It's still doing a sneaky gymnastics routine behind me.

Schnoodle Speak

God Forgives and Forgets Our Sin

Once God forgives our sin, He never thinks about it again. He is not like a human, who can remember it at another time. He never holds our sin against us. He erases it completely, then forgets about it. It is absolutely gone.

In Tucker's doggie world, the puffs of warm air hanging in the cold air of the ice cream parlor are like sin. When God forgives us, the air puffs, like sin, totally disappear. It vanishes forever and ever.

For I will forgive their wickedness and remember their sins no more. (Hebrews 8:12)

Takeaway: God forgets your sin permanently when you ask for forgiveness.

Chapter 5
Bathing Birds! Yuck!

My paws felt so nice and cool in the ice cream parlor, but now I have to hip hop on my toes over the hot cobblestones. Ouch, ouch, ouch! I'm like popcorn kernels popping!

I'm thirsty too!

My tongue feels like a dry, fuzzy bathmat in my mouth.

Oh good, there's the fountain in the middle of the town square. I set the packages carefully off to the side, remembering Molly will be extra cranky if I bring home scrambled cake and ice cream.

The water is clear, blue, and bubbling in the fountain. I scan for just the right place to drink and cool my hot paws. I jog around the fountain, searching for an open spot. I don't want to drink where the birds are bathing. Yuck! Who wants to drink a bird's bathwater?

I don't understand all that bathing. Who wants to be that clean? I only go to the groomer when I get tricked into it! I love my doggie smell, but when I go to the groomer, they take it away! Then I need to start all over and collect all my favourite smells again in my fur. The only good part about the groomer is the new bowtie or bandana that I get.

Oh! A clear space back where I started! Jumping onto the ledge around the fountain, I slurp a long, cool drink.

My tongue rolls back up into my mouth. *Whew!* That's much better!

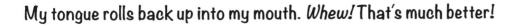

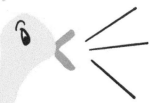

Keeping alert, my eyes wide, I listen to the birds. I understand a bit of bird talk, but it's never that interesting. Birdseed, birdseed, worms, birdseed, and the weather. They *love* talking about the weather. *Ugh!* I can't listen to another weather report!

Unable to resist the urge any longer, I leap into the water, splashing and scattering all those silly, feathery bathers! Feathers fly in all directions, and the water sloshes out of the fountain. Pleased and laughing so the birds can hear me, I think, *That will give them something to talk about!*

Gathering the boxes, I feel the strings slide between my teeth, flossing out the last bit of cherry. That was a yummy surprise! Between the cherry bonus and scattering the birds, this has been an excellent stop! I prance toward the party decoration store.

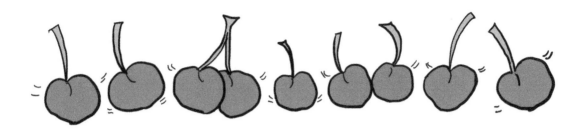

I pay no attention to my sly, pink sidekick that is secretly trailing me like an undercover agent.

We Will Sin Again

It doesn't matter how hard we try, we will sin again. It may be the same sin or a different one. This is because we are not perfect. Even if we don't want to sin, eventually we will slip up and sin again.

In Tucker's doggie world, his doggie smell is like sin. His smell collects in his fur, and it needs to be washed away by the groomer. Once the groomer thoroughly washes Tucker's fur with bubbling shampoo, he is fresh and clean. Sin, like doggie smell, is bad. If sin is left unforgiven, it stinks and can become a bad habit.

The problem is, when Tucker is squeaky clean, he will start collecting his doggie smell all over again. In time, he will need to go to the groomer to be scrubbed clean. We are the same way. We will sin again and need God's forgiveness. He is waiting to forgive us every time of every sin. Sometimes sins are called transgressions.

Save me from all my transgressions. (Psalm 39:8)

Takeaway: God forgives us over and over.

Chapter 6
Disguises and Decorations

Using my nose, I push open the door to the party decoration shop. A little bell lets the shop girl know I am here. It is like being in a colorful cloud. Balloons of all colors float above me like a bubbly rainbow.

Friendly streamers wave down from between the balloons. There are funny party hats, noisemakers, games, and gift bags with toys and treats.

What fun! I don't ever want to leave! Except Paul, Makaila, and Hannah would have to come live here too. They would love it! We could play hide and seek in here forever.

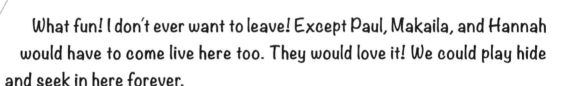

Gently, I set down Molly's packages and race to try on a hat. Barking excitedly, I come to a skidding stop with my back paws. First, I choose a tall hat striped in purple and green. Then a red one with polka dots and a big floppy flower. Next, I pick a hat that's covered in feathers, but it reminds me of the birds, and I quickly take it off. I also see glasses, mustaches, and rubber noses.

This place is amazing! The next time I decide to go through the kitchen garbage, I'm coming here first for a disguise. That way they will never know it's me!

"Hi Tucker!" the shop girl calls from behind the counter. She has a long, blonde ponytail. "See what you want for Molly's birthday party?" I wag my tail yes until my whole back-end shakes. Ponytail Girl laughs. I like making people laugh.

There are so many brightly colored balloons; I can't choose just one or two.

I run flying through the air and jump at the strings. I catch a purple string with a purple balloon, then a yellow string with a yellow balloon, a blue string with a blue balloon, then a green one, then an orange one, then a pink!

Ponytail Girl is still laughing. "Silly boy, Tucker. The balloons look like they are popping out of your snout!" *Chuckle, chuckle.* That is funny. I tilt my head to let her know I'm listening. Grabbing at brilliantly colored streamers, I gather all the decorations I need and head to the counter. Molly will be so surprised! Ponytail Girl ties the balloons onto my collar and puts the streamers in a bag with a handle. Taking my job seriously, I hold the streamer bag and lift the stringed boxes into my mouth.

This will take balance. Ponytail Girl giggles. "You're a goofy guy! *Don't float away now!*" she teases.

I think, *What a great idea! I'll come back to try that another day!* Safely, I take a step one slow paw at a time.

My gummy, gooey shoe is a springy accordion stretched as far as it will go. Its sticky paw prints are like a road map quietly left behind at every stop along my route.

Sometimes We Disguise Our Sin

There are times when we know that we are sinning. We like it and the way that it makes us feel, but do not want to admit it. Trying to disguise sin so it doesn't look or sound like sin makes us feel better about ourselves. We disguise sin by pretending that it's not too bad or it's not as bad as something else. Doing this helps us feel less guilty or bad. Secretly, we may even want to continue the sin because we enjoy it.

In Tucker's doggie world, his sin is going through the garbage. He does not want to give this sin up because he delights in the smells and tastes of the forbidden scraps. Tucker believes that if he puts on a rubber-nose disguise the next time he sins, nobody will know. That way he won't feel guilty either.

Tucker disguises his sin with an actual disguise. As people, we disguise our sin differently. No matter what the disguise is or how we explain it to ourselves, it is still sin. God sees all our sin, even through the disguises. There's nothing that is too bad for God to forgive.

God's son, Jesus, died on the cross for us and *all our sin*. Jesus died on the cross on Good Friday. He rose from the grave, or was resurrected, on Easter Sunday. Because He died and was resurrected, He has defeated and overcome *all* sin.

> The eyes of the Lord are everywhere, keeping watch on the wicked and the good. (Proverbs 15:3)

Takeaway: God sees all our sin, even through disguises. He will forgive *all* sin.

Chapter 7
A Reverse Trip!

I can smell that squirrel again, so good and stinky! I would love to chase him! *Oh,* and popcorn! That popcorn smells so yummy. I'm starved! I wish I had that doughnut hat right now!

Bending low, I creep under the crooked tree branches so I do not tangle the balloons. My secret mission is near the end. "Sargent Tucker is on the job," I mumble. "I will make sure the supplies get safely home."

I clear the hanging tree branches, then quickly dodge to the side to miss stepping on a fat, fuzzy caterpillar.

I catch my balance, the boxes swaying in my mouth. I can do this! I will make it to the other side of the park. The scent of the squirrel is stronger and stinkier. That little furball is close by. I sidestep, going wide around Popcorn Man and his cart full of delicious, buttery treats. Out of the corner of my eye, I see him! That sneaky squirrel! He laughs at me and zips past so close I can feel his breeze. The smell is so tempting, but I must resist. Duty calls! The supplies are almost home! I'll come back for that stinker later.

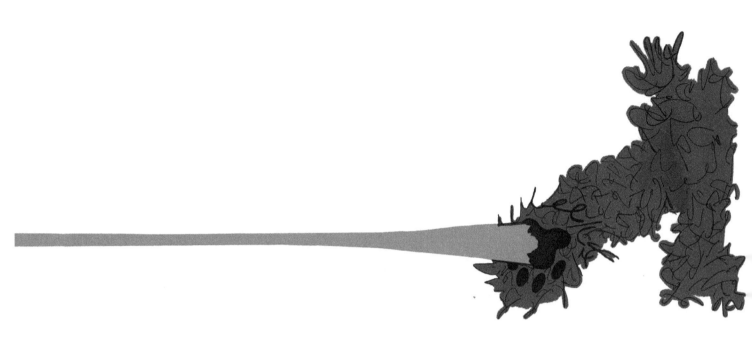

There's my house just ahead! I'm determined to deliver everything safely. My paw touches the cool cement of my front step when I hear a single *snap* in my ears. My bubble gum slipper has stretched its last stretch! It has gone as far as it can go, and now it wants to take me on a reverse trip! My furry body whirls through the air backward, ears flapping in the breeze.

I snap and pop my way through the party decoration shop.

I water-ski around the fountain and scatter all the birds.

I skate through the ice cream parlor.

In and out, in and out, in and out. I thump through the steps of the firefighter's ladder.

Splat, splat, splat. I collide with the yummy cakes as I travel through the bakery.

I whip all the way back through the park and land in a tangled mess of pink bubble gum, ice cream, popcorn, and cake! The balloons and streamers are spun around me and floating off my pointy ears, paws, and tail! All the noise awakens Molly from her lazy nap. She opens her eyes wide, wide, wider!

"Wow!" she says. "A pinata for my birthday!"

Ignoring Our Sin

If we choose not to ask God for forgiveness and ignore our sin instead, it can take us down harmful paths. It can pull us into messes and bad habits. It can ruin our friendships, and even our relationships with our parents or guardians. Sin is like a sneaky ninja who is always waiting to trap us.

In Tucker's doggie world, the stretching bubble gum is like unforgiven sin. It trails Tucker and is part of his life everywhere he goes. When it snaps, Tucker experiences everything and every place it has touched. Sin is like that too. It can move through every part of our lives without us knowing. Ultimately, it can land us in a tangled heap of trouble, just like Tucker.

Afterward, we may need to clean up the messes that we have made. We may have to break bad habits, ask others for forgiveness, and fix broken friendships.

You may be sure that your sin will find you out. (Numbers 32:23)

Takeaway: Leaving sin unconfessed is like a pebble that becomes a boulder.

THERE'S A PARTY!

To: You
LOVE: GOD
WHERE: HEAVEN
WHEN: FOREVER + EVER

There is an amazing party going on in heaven, and you are invited! This party is happening right now and will continue for all eternity, forever and ever. God loves you with a deep, pure love that will never change or disappear. He created you as a precious, one-of-a-kind person. God sees you as loveable, worthwhile, and important. He will never leave you or give up on you. He wants to be the Lord of your life and your friend forever.

If you want to reply yes to God's invitation, it is very easy. Pray the following prayer out loud: "God, thank you for sending Jesus to die on the cross for me and my sins. Please forgive me of my sins. Jesus, I invite you to come into my heart forever. Amen."

See you at the party!

TUCKER'S BRAIN
TEASERS

Reading Questions:

1. Who is Lou? Look carefully at pages 6 and 76.
2. Why did Tucker think there were no actual tigers in tiger ice cream?
3. What does Tucker think the air in the park smells like?
4. What is on top of the birthday cake?
5. How many balloons are illustrated in the book? Add them all up!
6. Why does Tucker want to go back to the party decoration shop another day?
7. How many times does Tucker walk through the park?
8. What kind of dog is Dottie?
9. What is the Schnoodelizer 2000?
10. What do the birds talk about at the fountain?

Answers:

1. Lou is the mouse who lives in a hole in Tucker's house. He has a welcome mat with his name on it, page 6. He is sleeping on a piece of birthday cake, page 76.
2. Cats don't like the cold.
3. Popcorn and squirrels.
4. Molly's name in purple icing.
5. Eighty-eight. This includes the balloons on the birthday list, page 6.
6. To get more balloons to see if he can float.
7. Twice: the first time going into town and the second time going home. The other times he is flying through the air!
8. Dalmatian.
9. A pasta spoon to stir pasta.
10. Birdseed, worms, and the weather.

The Barkery

Human's Birthday Cake

Serves 8

1 cup salted butter (½ pound)
1 cup white granulated sugar
1 cup packed brown sugar
2 eggs, beaten
2 teaspoons vanilla extract
2 and ¼ cups packed all-purpose flour
¾ cup cocoa (I use Fry's)
1 teaspoon salt
2 teaspoons baking powder
1 teaspoon baking soda
1 cup whole milk (you can use skim)
1 cup very hot water

Preheat oven to 325 degrees F. Place the rack in the middle position. Grease two 7.5 x 7.5 inches (19 cm x 19 cm) round cake pans and set aside.

Place the butter in a bowl or measuring cup in the microwave for about one minute to melt. Set the melted butter on the kitchen counter to cool.

Mix the white sugar and brown sugar in a large mixing bowl. Mix in the eggs and vanilla.

Cup your hands around the bowl containing the melted butter. (Tucker's Tip: Do not check if the butter is cool enough with your tongue!) If the bowl or measuring cup containing the melted butter is cool enough to hold in your hands comfortably for 5 seconds, then it's cool enough so it won't cook the eggs. Stir it into your mixing bowl.

Using an electric mixer on medium speed, mix thoroughly. (Tucker's Tip: You will need super strong muscles to mix all the ingredients by hand. If you have an electric mixer, it is easier.) The mixture should be light and fluffy.

In a separate medium bowl, combine the flour, salt, baking powder, baking soda, and cocoa. Mix together with a spoon and set aside.

Pour milk into a measuring cup and set aside.

Let your kitchen tap run until the water is very hot. Measure the very hot water carefully into a measuring cup and set aside. (Tucker's Tip: Make sure an adult is helping so you don't burn a paw. I mean a hand!)

Add half of the flour mixture to the light, fluffy mixture in your large bowl. This is your main mixing bowl. Mix on medium speed until completely combined.

Add half of the very hot water to the main mixing bowl. Mix until smooth and combined. (Tucker's Tip: Place a kitchen towel over the electric mixer while mixing because sometimes the water splashes. Ouch!)

Add half of the milk to the main mixing bowl. Mix until smooth and combined.

Repeat these steps, adding the other half of the flour mixture, hot water, and then the milk.

Scrape down the sides of bowl and give the contents a stir by hand with a spatula or a spoon.

Evenly distribute the cake batter between the two well-greased, round cake pans until they are both three-quarters full.

Bake for 55 minutes, or until you test it and it's done. You can test your cake to see if it's baked all the way by using a toothpick, a cake tester, or a butter knife. If you insert it one inch from the center of the cake, it should come out clean with no batter sticking to it. If it doesn't, bake your cake in extra 5-minute increments until your tester comes out clean. Remove the cake from the oven.

Let the cake cool in the pans on a wire rack. Once completely cooled, turn the pans upside down so the cake falls out. If the cake sticks, loosen the edges by running a butter knife between the cake and the pan's edge.

Frost with your choice of icing.

Peanut Butter Snicker Snackers

Tucker's personal favorite!

Makes approximately 45 small cookies

½ cup bacon bits (Tucker likes Hormel Real Bacon Bits)
½ cup peanut butter (Kraft Crunchy Peanut Butter is Tucker's favorite)
1 egg, beaten
1 and ¼ cups all-purpose flour, divided
¼ cup water

Preheat the oven to 325 degrees F. Place the rack in the middle position. Line a large cookie sheet with parchment paper or tin foil and set aside.

In a large mixing bowl, stir together the bacon bits, peanut butter, and egg until completely combined.

Add ½ cup of flour and mix until completely combined. Then add the other ½ cup of flour and mix until completely combined.

Add the water and mix until blended. The dough may be a bit sticky, but you should be able to gather it into a ball. It should feel a little like Play-Doh.

Lightly sprinkle ⅛ cup of flour onto a clean counter. Place the dough on the floured countertop. Sprinkle the top of the dough with the remaining ⅛ cup flour. (Tucker's Tip: This prevents the dough from sticking to the counter and the rolling pin. You can use a little less or a little more if you need to.)

Using a rolling pin, roll the dough to approximately ½ -inch (0.6cm) thickness. Use cookie cutter shapes to make your fur friend a delicious snack! (Tucker's Tip: I love the bone shapes!)

Place cutout cookies on the large parchment or tin foil-lined cookie sheet. They do not spread-out during baking, so you can put them close together.

Bake for thirty-five minutes. Cool completely on the pan.

The cookies will keep at room temperature in an airtight container for 7–10 days.

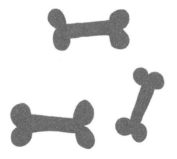

About My Owner

(The Author)

Jill enjoys spending time with Tucker, laughing at his silly antics, and translating his adventures as he relays them to her!

Jill has a deep love and compassion for all children. She has a certificate in early childhood development. As a preschool teacher, she could often be found vividly telling stories with different voices in her classroom. She has created and developed Christian curriculum with evangelistic outreach for children. She is also the co-author and illustrator of *Tucker Goes to City Hall*, a book for elementary children about municipal government.

Schnoodle Shenanigans! is a passion project that can be used to teach children about God's character, biblical concepts, and to relay the salvation message to young people. Our time is short; He is coming soon!

Printed in the USA
CPSIA information can be obtained
at www.ICGtesting.com
LVHW060415230524
780645LV00003B/24